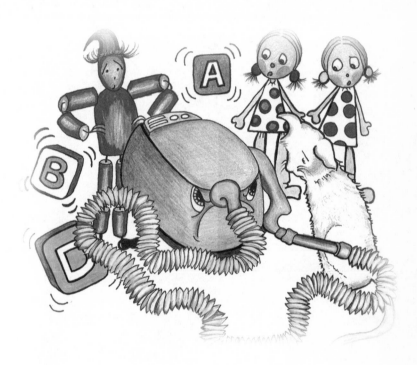

To

Dominic Mason

The Fed-Up Vacuum Cleaner

Written by

Cora Harrison

Illustrated by Ruth Ryan

MENTOR
BOOKS

This Edition first published 2002 by

MENTOR BOOKS
43 Furze Road,
Sandyford Industrial Estate,
Dublin 18.

Tel. (01) 295 2112/3   Fax. (01) 295 2114
e-mail: admin@mentorbooks.ie
www.mentorbooks.ie

ISBN: 1-84210-148-X

A catalogue record for this book is available from
the British Library

Cover and Illustrations: Ruth Ryan
Editing, Design and Layout by Mentor Books

Printed in Ireland by ColourBooks Ltd.

1 3 5 7 9 10 8 6 4 2

The little vacuum cleaner was fed up.

'No one ever thinks about me,'
said the vacuum cleaner.

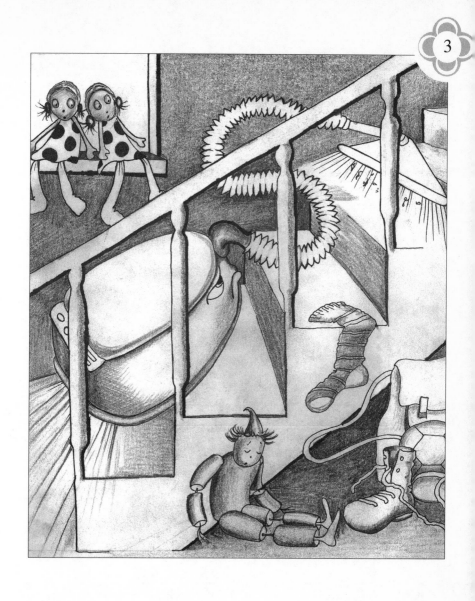

'All I do is work, work, work.'

'And gobble spiders.'

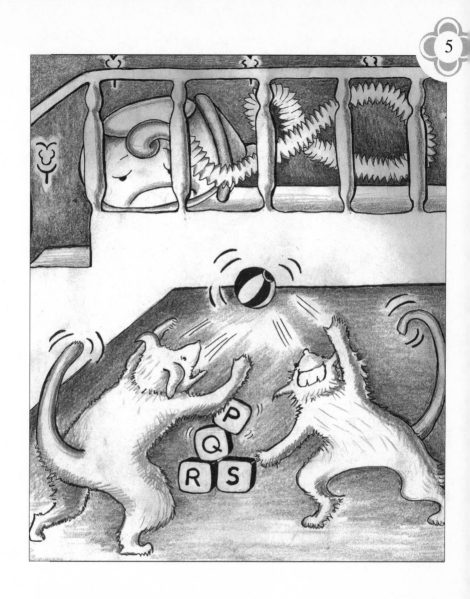

'I have no friends,' said the little vacuum cleaner.

'I never go anywhere nice like school,'
said the little vacuum cleaner.

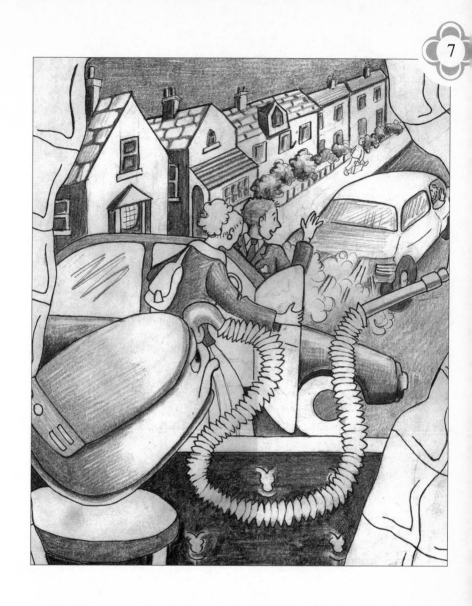

'I never go out to work.'

'I know what I'll do,' said the
little vacuum cleaner.

'I'll run away.'

'I'll find a nice school for vacuum cleaners with lots of nice friendly vacuum cleaners to play with.'

'Or a vacuum cleaner office
with lots of friends.'

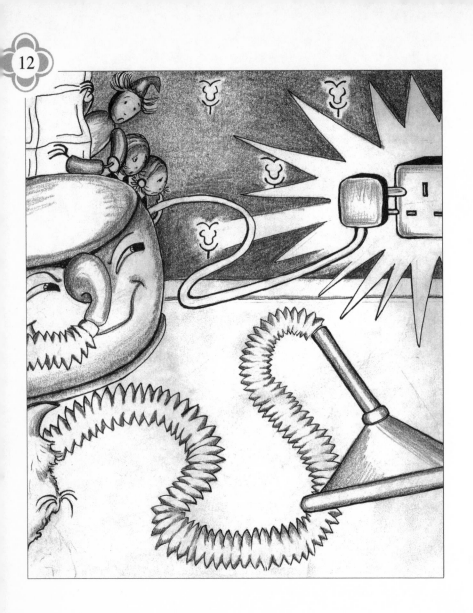

'But first I'll have some fun. It's time for me to make a mess.'

'Floors first,' said the little
vacuum cleaner.

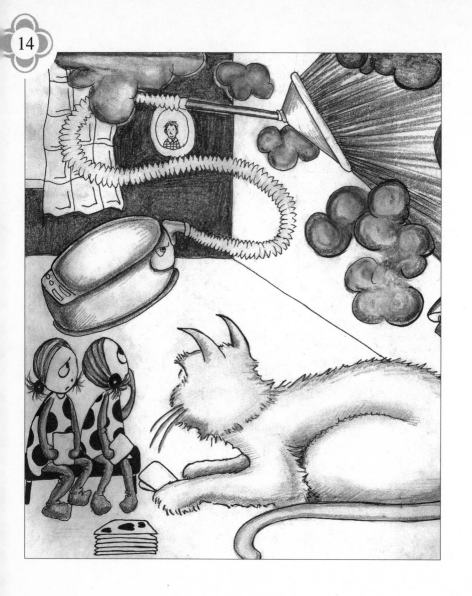

'Walls next,' said the little
vacuum cleaner.

'Now the stairs.'

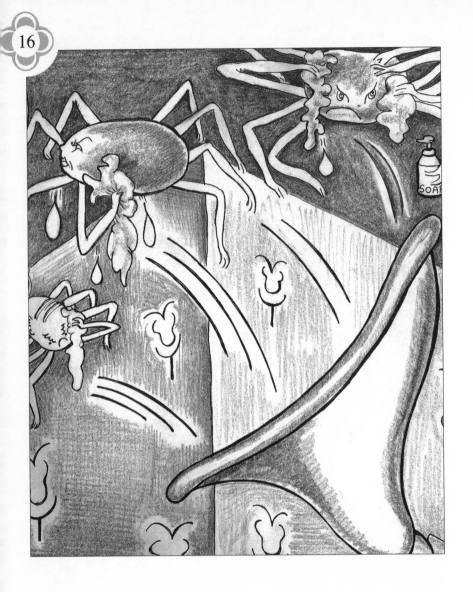

'Now for a few spiders,' said the little vacuum cleaner.

'Now I'm off.'

'You're nothing but a slave,' said the vacuum cleaner to the road cleaner.

'Will you please tell me where
the school for vacuum cleaners
is?' asked the vacuum cleaner.

'Why do people leave rubbish lying around in the streets?' said the traffic warden.

'This looks like a nice place,'
said the little vacuum cleaner.

'Get that vacuum cleaner out of
here,' said a very cross man.

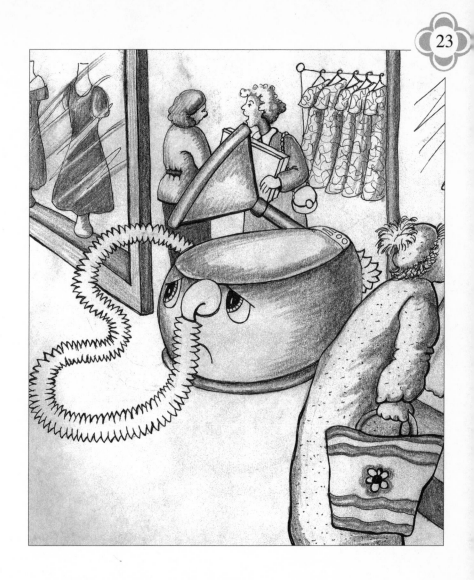

'What a cross man,' said the
little vacuum cleaner sadly. 'He
won't be a good friend for me.'

'This smells nice,' said the little
vacuum cleaner.

'It looks nice and clean too.
There'll be no hard work for me
here.'

'I'll have to get that vacuum cleaner out of here,' said a cross woman.

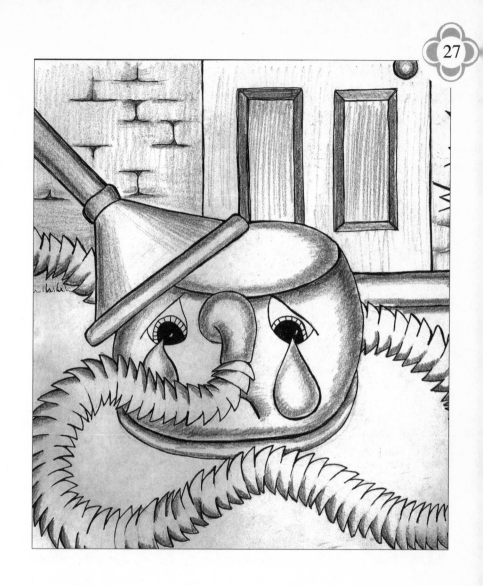

'Oh dear,' said the little vacuum cleaner sadly. 'No one seems to like vacuum cleaners here.'

The sad little vacuum cleaner
walked down the street.

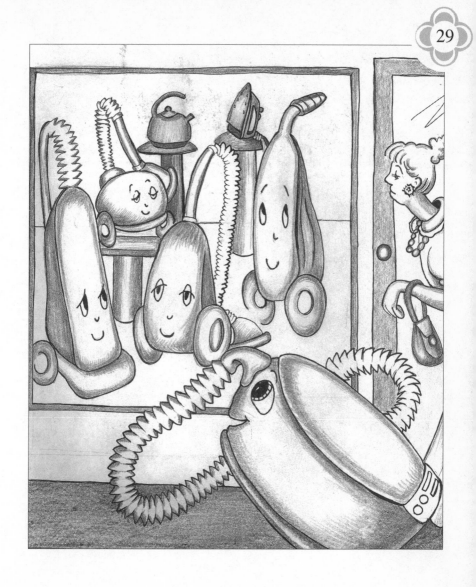

'Oh look,' he said. 'This is a school for vacuum cleaners.'

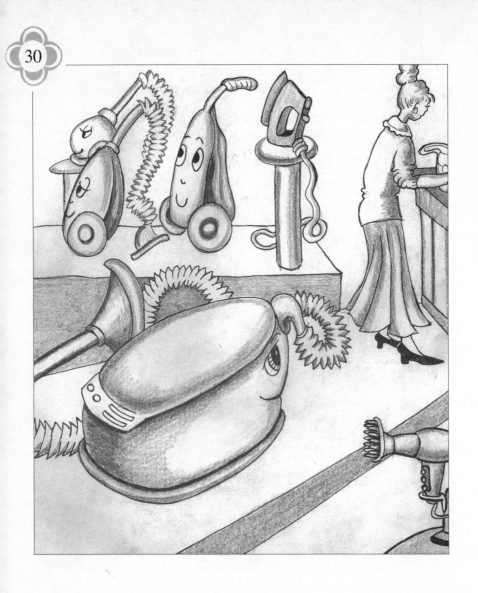

The little vacuum cleaner went
into the shop. He stood next to
a big black vacuum cleaner.

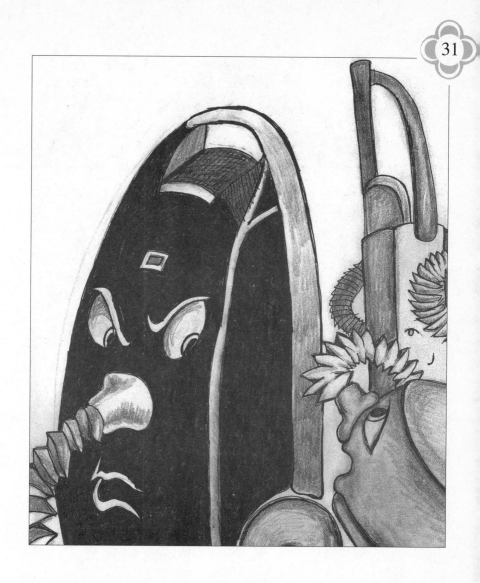

'Will you be my friend?' he asked.

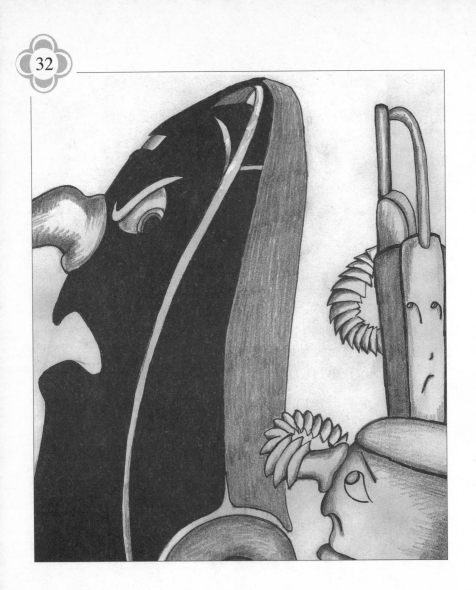

'No,' said the big black vacuum cleaner. 'I only make friends with new vacuum cleaners.'

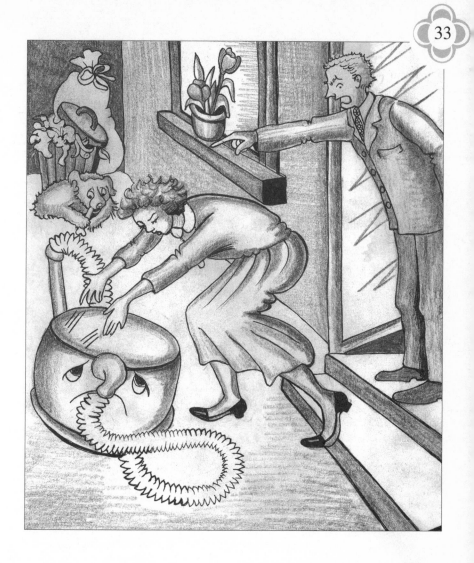

'Get that old vacuum cleaner out of here,' shouted the cross shop man.

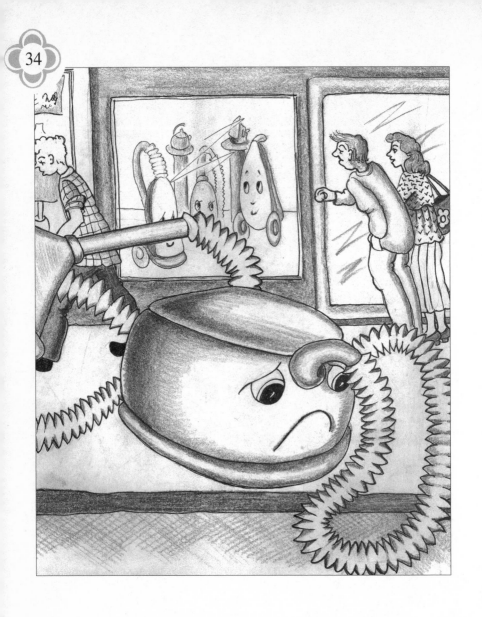

'I think I'll go home,' said the
little vacuum cleaner sadly.

'Who made that mess?' said Dad.

'It wasn't us, Dad!'

'Oh, no' said Dad. 'The little
vacuum cleaner is not here.
We need to find it soon.'

'Thank goodness! Here it is,'
said Dad.

'Quick, Dad, Mum's coming!'

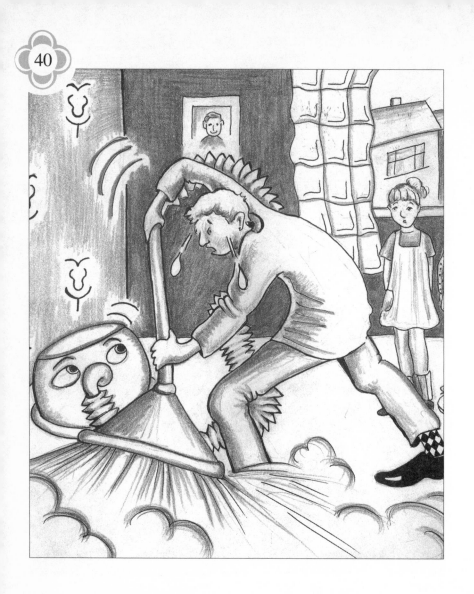

'First the floors, and now the walls,' said Dad. 'This is a great little vacuum cleaner.'

'What would we do without you, little vacuum cleaner?' said Dad.

'Machines are great,' said Dad.
'I'll buy this one for washing
the floors. Mum will like that.'

'Well, the house looks nice
and clean,' said Mum.

'Well, it's nice to be home
again,' said the vacuum
cleaner. 'And it will be very
nice to have a friend.'